COSTUMES FOR COLORING

Kings & Queens
Around the World

Illustrated by Jenny Williams
Text by Laura Driscoll

Grosset & Dunlap • New York

KINGS & QUEENS AROUND THE WORLD features fascinating monarchs from every corner of the globe. Queen Elizabeth I of England, Tsar Nicholas II of Russia, the Hawaiian King Kamehameha and many more emperors and empresses, shahs, and sultans parade one after another through this majestic coloring book.

Each page in KINGS & QUEENS AROUND THE WORLD opens a window onto the lives and times of some of the most powerful men and women in history. The clear, accurately detailed drawings are printed back-to-back with often surprising information about the lifestyles, quirks, and costumes of each ruler. This way, a colored page can be removed with the fun, informative notes still attached.

This unique book offers the double pleasures of creative coloring and exploring world history through some of its most "colorful" personalities.

Elizabeth I, Queen of England (1558-1603)

Elizabeth's reign, often called the Golden Age or the Elizabethan Age, was a peaceful and prosperous time for the English. The navy grew strong enough to challenge the most powerful fleets in the world, while at the same time, Elizabeth managed to avoid war with many of her enemies. Known as "Good Queen Bess," she is truly one of the most well-loved and respected monarchs in all of English history. This is certainly part of the reason why she was such a role model and trendsetter in her day. Elizabeth's trademark wide and lacy ruff collar became very popular during her reign, even though she tried to pass laws forbidding her subjects to imitate her style. And when she started using thick white makeup later in her life, that caught on as well. Unfortunately, the makeup contained lead, and it eventually ruined Elizabeth's skin, as well as the skin of thousands of her subjects.

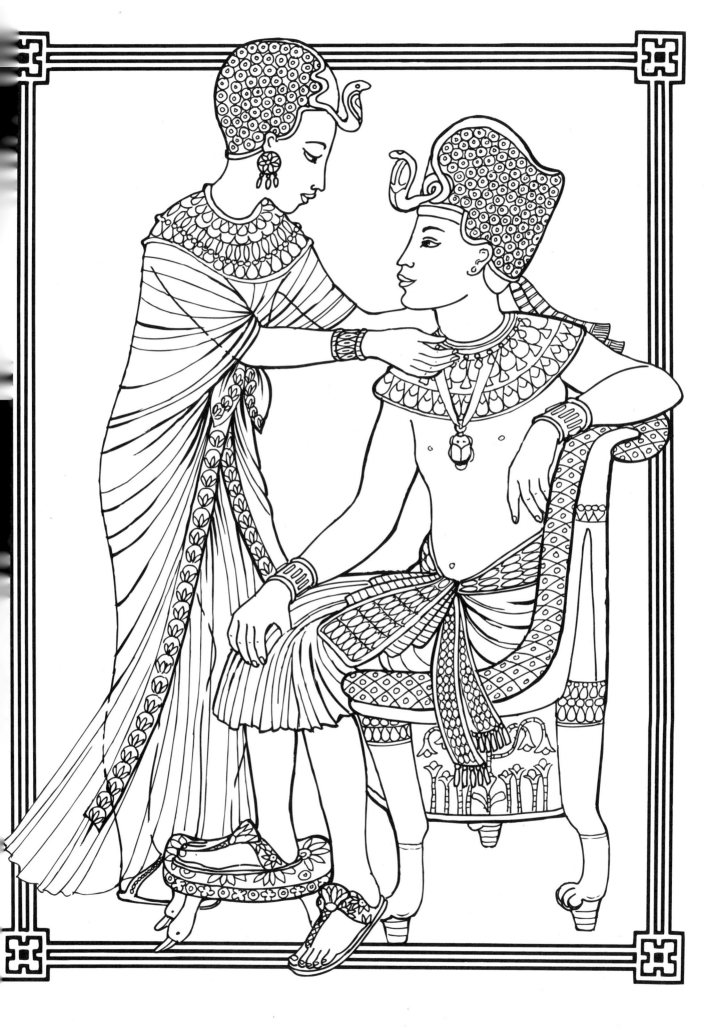

Tutankhamen and Ankhesenamen, Pharaoh and Queen of Egypt (1333-1323 B.C.)

Tutankhamen was not an important ruler during his lifetime, but the discovery of his treasure-filled tomb in 1922 made him the most well-known Egyptian pharaoh of modern times. Historians can't be sure, but many believe that King Tut was adopted. His mother, Nefertiti, who was queen before Tut took the throne, had no sons and feared that her enemies would seize power after she died. No one really knows where Nefertiti found Tutankhamen, but at the age of eight, he became the ruler of Egypt and took his adopted sister, Ankhesenamen, as his queen.

Pharaohs, like all Egyptians, tried to stay cool by wearing loose-fitting clothing made from lightweight fabric. Formal temple dress was a short kilt under a sheer overskirt, a modified war helmet, and slippers with images of the pharaoh's enemies painted on the soles so he could step on their likenesses every day.

Justinian and Theodora,
Emperor and Empress of Byzantium (527-565)

Emperor Justinian ruled the Byzantine Empire when it was at its largest: Italy, Greece, Asia Minor, and parts of North Africa, Spain, and the Middle East were all under his control. When Justinian married at the age of forty-three, he surprised everyone with his choice. Instead of picking from among Byzantium's richest noblewomen, he chose Theodora, a peasant who had worked as an actress, dancer, and wool spinner! Theodora's father was a bear keeper at the zoo in Constantinople. Before the couple could wed, Justinian had to change Byzantine law to allow marriages between nobles and peasants.

Wealthy Byzantines loved to wear silk, but until the 500s, it had to be imported from Persia and China. Then, during Justinian's reign, two Persian monks smuggled some silkworms out of China and delivered them to the emperor. Now the Byzantines could make their own silk, and the fashions of the empire changed forever.

Nicholas II and Alexandra, Tsar and Tsarina of Russia (1894-1917)

Nicholas and Alexandra had only one son, a boy named Alexis, who was the heir to the Russian crown. Alexis suffered from a very dangerous blood disease called hemophilia. If Alexis got a cut or scrape, nothing could stop the bleeding. Nicholas and Alexandra worried about their son. Doctors had not been able to help, but a mysterious monk named Rasputin had a strange ability to control Alexis's illness. Rasputin was feared and distrusted by most Russians. He and his followers did not seem very holy, and many believed they were downright evil. As Rasputin grew closer to the tsar and his family, the Russian people lost faith in their leader. Military losses and food shortages led to even more unhappiness among the people, and the Russian Revolution began. During the revolution, the Russians overthrew the system of rule by tsars.

Shah Jahan, Emperor of India (1628-1658)

Shah Jahan had been designing palaces and forts since the age of sixteen. But when his wife died while giving birth to their fourteenth child, Jahan wanted to build something fantastic in her memory. One of the most expensive and beautiful tombs in the world was the result—the Taj Mahal. It took more than 20,000 men working twenty-one years to complete. And when it was finally done, Shah Jahan had only more hardship to face. His own son overthrew him and locked him in a fort across the river from the Taj Mahal, where he gazed sadly out the window at his wife's tomb. After his death in 1666, Shah Jahan's body was rowed back across the river and put to rest beside her.

Otumfuo Opuku Ware II,
Asantehene of Ghana (1945-)

The asantehene, or king, of Ghana is honored every forty-two days at the *adae* festival. The king's attendants parade through the streets carrying gold staffs topped by the asantehene's symbol: a hand holding an egg, representing the ruler's care and patience. Both citizens and foreign visitors bring him gifts of rams and cows. But during the two-day festival, the asantehene himself is more concerned with honoring and remembering the rulers that came before him.

Louis XIV and Marie-Thérèse,
King and Queen of France (1643-1715)

Becoming a king at four years old can have its advantages. For Louis XIV, it meant an amazingly long reign of seventy-two years. Louis had plenty of time to build Versailles, one of the largest and most extravagant palaces in the world. Versailles has more than 1,000 fountains, marble walls and floors, and beautiful chandeliers, but not a single toilet and only a few bathtubs. However, the king and his guests didn't mind. Although they wore the finest silk, velvet, and lace, they didn't like to bathe. They always chose perfume over soap and water.

What the king *did* mind was being disappointed by the servants. Once, while preparing food for a large dinner party, the palace chef was short of lobsters for a special sauce. Rather than admit this to the king, the chef committed suicide.

Ahmed III, Sultan of the Ottoman Empire (1703-1730)

A sultan who ruled many years before Ahmed III introduced a way to prevent members of the royal family from fighting over power. Called "the Cage," it was a group of rooms in the palace in which all male relatives of the ruling sultan were held prisoner. This way, they couldn't try to take over. These men spent the rest of their lives under lock and key, unless the sultan died and someone was needed to replace him. Those who *were* lucky enough to be released sometimes came out completely insane, and the empire ended up with a crazy ruler. Apparently, however, the Cage wasn't always effective, because in 1703, Ahmed stole power from his brother, Mustafa II. And in 1730, Ahmed's own nephew overthrew him.

Chu Yu-t'ang and Chang,
Emperor and Empress of the Ming Dynasty,
China (1488-1506)

Chu Yu-t'ang is known as the most kind and humane emperor of the Ming Dynasty. In the first few months of his reign, he fired and demoted many government officials who had bribed their way to the top. He almost never lost his temper, and even when an official offended him or broke the law, Chu Yu-t'ang refused to beat him in public or use any other cruel methods of punishment. More than anything else, however, Chu Yu-t'ang is remembered for being completely faithful to his wife, Empress Chang. He was probably the first emperor in the history of imperial China for whom this is true.

The emperor's ordinary dress, shown here, was called the "dragon robe." It was made of yellow satin and was embroidered with dragon patterns and pheasant designs. Empress Chang is shown in ceremonial dress, wearing the phoenix crown. The crown was a framework of wires, on which an imitation phoenix, pearls, and precious stones were mounted.

Grace Kelly, Princess of Monaco (1956-1982)

Born and raised in Philadelphia, Grace Kelly packed up and moved to New York City as a teenager to try her luck as a model and actress. And the risk paid off. She starred in some of the most popular movies of the mid-1950s, and won an Academy Award in 1954 for her performance in *The Country Girl*. Although she starred with some of Hollywood's most handsome leading men (including Clark Gable, Cary Grant, and Jimmy Stewart), she did not find the man of her dreams until she was introduced to Prince Rainier of Monaco while he was in the United States for a magazine interview. America was enchanted by their romance. On Grace's wedding day, U.S. newspaper headlines read, "Hollywood Princess Weds Real-Life Prince."

Saud Aziz, Emir of Saudi Arabia (1953-1964)

Oil was discovered in Saudi Arabia in 1938, and by 1950, the Middle Eastern country was making about $1 million every week in sales of oil to other nations. Oil had made Saudi Arabia a very wealthy country, indeed. The king, Emir Saud, obviously thought there was money to burn. He built many extravagant palaces, and he rode around in his Rolls-Royce, tossing gold coins out the window to the penniless Bedouins who roamed the deserts. The rest of the royal family thought Saud's wasteful behavior was in bad taste. In 1964, they forced him to step aside and give the throne over to his younger brother.

Louis XVI and Marie-Antoinette, King and Queen of France (1774-1789)

King Louis XVI, Marie-Antoinette, and all of the court lived in such luxury and spent so much of France's money that the country almost went bankrupt in the 1780s. Marie-Antoinette aroused the French people's anger by spending ridiculous amounts of money on jewels and extravagant costumes trimmed with ermine, lace, pearls, and gold. Taxes went way up—the king wanted his subjects to pay off his tremendous debt. By 1789, however, the citizens had had enough and raised a revolt to overthrow the monarchy. Louis and his family, in an attempt to escape from France, disguised themselves and headed for the border. But in the end, they were recognized by a soldier in Belgium, taken back to Paris, and beheaded. How did the soldier know what the king looked like? From his picture on French money, of course!

Hadj Halidon Sali, Lamido of Bibemi, Cameroon

Today there are over twenty-one Lamibe (plural of Lamido) in Cameroon, a country about the size of California on the west coast of Africa. But the role of the Lamibe has changed very much over the past thirty years. Before the election of Cameroon's first president, Ahmadou Ahidjo, in the early 1960s, the Lamibe held all religious, judicial, and political power over their kingdoms. But President Ahidjo passed laws that took away most of the Lamibe's powers. According to the law, they are now simply religious leaders. They can no longer impose taxes or have use of the police force. But in reality, the Lamibe often have more influence and power than the government would like.

Ashurbanipal, King of Assyria (668-627 B.C.)

Ashurbanipal was the last great king of the Assyrians. During his reign, Assyria was the most powerful nation in the world. His empire grew to include Babylonia, Persia, Syria, and Egypt. He was a dreaded warrior, but Ashurbanipal also had a great appreciation for art and literature. He collected a library of over 22,000 clay tablets containing writings of ancient Sumerians, Babylonians, and Assyrians, and stored them all in the palace library. Whether he knew it or not, Ashurbanipal was doing a great service for later historians. Today, Ashurbanipal's library is safe and sound in the British Museum. It is, by far, the best guide to the history of ancient Assyria in existence.

Maria Theresa, Empress of Austria (1740-1780)

Maria Theresa's father, Emperor Charles, had no sons, and had to make a special law allowing a woman to take the throne so that his daughter could rule Austria. Rulers of neighboring countries thought they would be able to take advantage of a female. But Maria Theresa proved herself to be a very strong military leader and an outstanding empress in many ways. Music thrived with her help and support—Mozart, Haydn, and Beethoven all lived in Vienna during her reign. Mozart, already displaying his musical genius, met the empress when he was only six years old. He even got to sit in her lap! Haydn wasn't so lucky. He was very naughty as a young choirboy in Vienna, and one story suggests that the empress herself ordered that Haydn be spanked for his bad behavior.

Rama IV (1851-1868) and Rama V (1868-1910), Kings of Thailand

Without a doubt, Rama V—shown here as a boy—was the king who modernized Thailand and brought the country into the twentieth century. He abolished slavery, introduced electric lighting, and opened the first hospital. He built an electric tramcar system in Bangkok, and imported the first automobiles into the country almost as soon as they were invented. In fact, cars appeared on the streets of Bangkok very shortly after they appeared on the streets of American cities and towns. But Rama had a very tough act to follow. His father, King Rama IV, is known to American movie audiences as the lead character in *The King and I*. Based on a true story by an English schoolteacher, the film is still banned in Thailand because it portrays the real-life king in a negative light.

Henry VIII, Anne Boleyn, and Jane Seymour, King (1509-1547) and Queens (Anne Boleyn, 1533-1536; Jane Seymour, 1536-1537) of England

Queens did not last for very long around Henry VIII. Of his six wives, he had two killed and divorced two, while one died of natural causes. Only his last wife outlived him. Henry began his long string of marriages with Catherine of Aragon. All of Catherine's sons died while still infants. And Henry, more than anything, wanted a male heir. He asked for a divorce, but the Pope of the Roman Catholic Church, the religious leader of England at the time, said no. As a result, Henry rejected the Catholic Church and founded the Church of England. And he promptly divorced Catherine. Henry then married Anne Boleyn. But Anne bore a daughter, and Henry beheaded her after accusing her of being unfaithful to him. Henry finally got his heir with his next wife, Jane Seymour, who died shortly after giving birth to the son who would become King Edward VI.

Henry is shown here in a costume that is very typical of the early 1500s. The overall shape is broad and square, and the sleeves of his coat are "slashed"—a popular technique in which the outer layer of clothing was cut and the inner lining made to show through.

Fath 'Ali , Shah of Iran (1797-1834)

For the most part, Fath 'Ali's time on the throne was very peaceful and uneventful. It was only toward the end of his rule, in 1826, that Russia invaded Iran, attempting to gain more land and an outlet to the Persian Gulf. But even this conflict eventually ended peacefully when Russia was granted the land it wanted. Perhaps the quiet of Fath 'Ali's reign explains why he had enough time to wed more than 500 wives. Historians also estimate that the shah was the father of about 2,000 children.

Charlemagne, Holy Roman Emperor (800-814)

Charlemagne is the most famous ruler of the Middle Ages. He united most of western Europe under a great empire and revived European culture, which had collapsed along with the Roman Empire in the 400s. But Charlemagne earned himself quite a reputation as a fiercely religious ruler and very cruel conqueror. He vowed to convert the whole of his empire to Christianity—or kill everyone who objected. Kings and rulers of other nations, eager to win Charlemagne's favor, sent many gifts. One was a fully grown African elephant, which Charlemagne kept as a pet inside the palace.

Charlemagne tried to avoid formal dress as much as possible and preferred very simple clothing. For special occasions and ceremonies, however, Charlemagne typically wore several layers of painstakingly embroidered garments sewn with gold threads, heavily jeweled gloves, and the sapphire- and emerald-laden crown of the Holy Roman Empire.

Ashi Kesang and Ashi Dechen Waugmo,
Queen Mother and Princess of Bhutan (1973-)

The tiny nation of Bhutan is surrounded by India on three sides, with Tibet bordering to the north. Ashi Kesang and Ashi Dechen Waugmo are mother and sister to Bhutan's king, Jigme Singye Wangchuk, who struggles to protect Bhutan's values and culture while still guiding the country into the present. Jigme Singye is only the fourth "king" in Bhutan's history. Before 1907, the country was ruled by Shabdrungs, men who the Bhutanese people believed to be the reincarnations of the holy man who founded Bhutan. When King Jigme Singye was crowned in 1973, more than 150 foreign visitors were invited to the event. It was the first time the country was open to so many outsiders.

Kamehameha I and Kaahumanu,
King and Queen of Hawaii (1795-1819)

King Kamehameha I, the founding father of the "Kingdom of Hawaii," united all the Hawaiian islands under his rule. His queen is just as well known to Hawaiians. Although the king had many wives, Kaahumanu was his favorite and, at six feet and over 300 pounds, was considered the most beautiful woman in Hawaii. But if the stories about Kaahumanu are true, it's a wonder she made it to adulthood. It is said she was born in a cave on the island of Maui and that, as a baby, her cradle was swept out to sea and not even missed by her parents for a number of days!

Eugénie Marie de Montijo, Empress of France (1853-1870)

Louis Napoleon III (Napoleon I's brother) was very popular with the ladies—especially after he became emperor in 1852. Eugénie, a Spanish countess, set her sights on becoming his wife. She got herself invited to all the royal balls and, sure enough, Napoleon soon told her that he would ask for her hand in marriage. Unfortunately, Napoleon had forgotten that he had already proposed to someone else! Her name was Princess Adelaide, and she was Queen Victoria's niece. Luckily for Eugénie, Adelaide said no (maybe because she heard about Napoleon's second marriage proposal). Napoleon and Eugénie were married in 1853, and the beautiful empress became a style-setter for all of Europe.

Anak Agung Gde Anom,
Royal Prince of Karangasem, Bali

In the 1700s, Karangasem was the most powerful kingdom in all of Bali, a small island in the South Pacific. But today, Bali is ruled by the government of the Republic of Indonesia, and the once-powerful kingdom is gone. A little town called Amlapura stands where it once was. Tourists can still wander the grounds of the old Karangasem palaces in Amlapura, but they may not enter the buildings. Anak Agung Gde Anom and other members of the old royal family of Karangasem live quietly inside. Anom works as a schoolteacher, but the people of Amlapura still recognize and treat him like a royal prince.

Ranavalona III, Queen of Madagascar (1883-1896)

Ranavalona became queen of Madagascar, an island off the southeastern coast of Africa, in 1883. And in the same year, Ranavalona married the prime minister, a man named Rainilaiarivony. It was probably not a coincidence that the prime minister had also been married to the two preceding queens, and had been a prime suspect in the murder of Ranavalona's father. Rainilaiarivony was obviously grasping at power in every way that he could. And when the French seized control of Madagascar in 1895, they must have seen that he—and not the queen—was the real threat, because the prime minister was forced into exile. Ranavalona was allowed to remain on the throne as a figurehead, after signing a treaty that surrendered the island's independence to France.

Nezahualpilli, Aztec ruler of Texcoco (1472-1516)

The Aztecs built a mighty empire in Mexico during the 1400s and 1500s. Nezahualpilli ruled the Aztec city of Texcoco just before the Spanish invaded in 1519 and conquered his people. Many Aztecs believed that Nezahualpilli was more than a ruler. They thought he had the powers of a god and that he had predicted the arrival of the Spaniards. And even though the official records say he died in 1516, his subjects believed he would live forever. But some Aztecs feared Nezahualpilli's powers. His enemies said he had a pact with the devil, and they may have had a point. He executed his wife and two of his children when their behavior displeased him.

William II and Mary I,
King and Queen of the Netherlands (1647-1650)

In 1641, Mary, daughter of King Charles I of England, married Prince William, heir to the Dutch crown. On their wedding day, William was only fifteen years old; his bride was ten. And before they knew it, they had become the king and queen of the Netherlands. But their rule did not last very long. In 1650, at the age of twenty-four, William caught smallpox and died, leaving Mary alone and pregnant with their child. Strangely, William's death had been predicted. A few years before his death, an unknown woman presented William's mother with a horoscope for her son. It foretold that he would die in his twenty-fourth year, and a widow would give birth to his only child.

Khai Dinh, Emperor of Annam (1916-1925)

The kingdom of Annam was once located in a region of southeast Asia that today lies partially in North Vietnam and partially in South Vietnam. It was conquered by the Chinese in 214 B.C., but eventually won its own independence in 1428. The decline of Annam's power began in the late 1700s, when the French invaded. Throughout the 1800s, and during Emperor Khai Dinh's reign, the French gained more and more control over Annam. Khai Dinh was criticized by many of his subjects for not being more resistant to the French takeover.

Napoleon and Josephine,
Emperor and Empress of France (1804-1815)

Often called the greatest military genius of his time, Napoleon built an empire that covered most of western and central Europe. Napoleon won battle after battle, and gained so much popularity among the French people that he was able to declare himself emperor of France in 1804. At his coronation, he snatched the crown from the Pope and placed it on his head himself, to show that he had earned the right to be emperor. He then crowned his wife, Empress Josephine. Napoleon was eventually exiled after leading the French army on a doomed invasion of Russia in the dead of winter. He spent six years on a lonely island in the South Atlantic before he died in 1821. Although his death certificate lists cancer as the cause of his death, a Swedish dentist in the 1950s found very high levels of arsenic in samples of Napoleon's hair. This suggests that he may have been poisoned.

Victoria, Queen of England (1837-1901)

During Victoria's reign, the longest in English history, England built up a huge empire around the world and made many modern advances at home. Victoria is one of the most famous rulers in British history, and she was very popular among her subjects even before she officially became queen. Everyone wanted to see her crowning. "Coronation Madness" took hold of London—hotels were full, and there was not a single empty seat on trains and coaches into the city. Many people camped out overnight in the public parks. Victoria wrote in her diary that the noise of the people, the bands, and the other preparations woke her at four o'clock in the morning on Coronation Day.

A new crown had to be made for Victoria, since the crown worn by the kings before her was too heavy. A large heart-shaped ruby, diamonds, and other precious stones were moved from the old crown to the new one, and more diamonds, pearls, and a sapphire were added.

Hirohito and Nagako,
Emperor and Empress of Japan (1926-1989)

Although Emperor Hirohito was the 124th ruler in a line which goes all the way back to ancient Japan, he was the very first Japanese emperor ever to venture outside of the country during his reign. And Hirohito broke with Japanese tradition in other ways as well. Japanese emperors held a great amount of power during several periods in Japan's history. But in 1946, Hirohito placed all political power in the hands of elected representatives and declared himself just a symbol of the country. He also allowed photographs to be taken of the royal family, something that had always been forbidden. He hired American tutors to educate his son, Akhito, and he broke a centuries-old tradition when he permitted Akhito to marry a woman who was not a member of one of Japan's noble families.

Philip I and Juana,
King (1504-1506) and Queen (1504-1555) of Spain

Philip and Juana became king and queen of Spain when, in 1504, Juana inherited the throne from her mother, Queen Isabella—the very same Queen Isabella who paid for Christopher Columbus's 1492 trip across the Atlantic. Philip died in 1506. Juana was brokenhearted, and she was obviously not willing to say good-bye to her husband. She toured all of Spain with his coffin, and even took Philip's corpse with her when she retired to the countryside in 1509! She became widely known as Juana the Mad. Her son, Charles, became king in 1517 with Juana's permission. Officially, mother and son ruled together until Juana died in 1555. In reality, however, Juana was too depressed to do anything but mourn for her husband.